The Grown-up Trap

Ib Spang Olsen

Thomasson-Grant
Charlottesville, Virginia

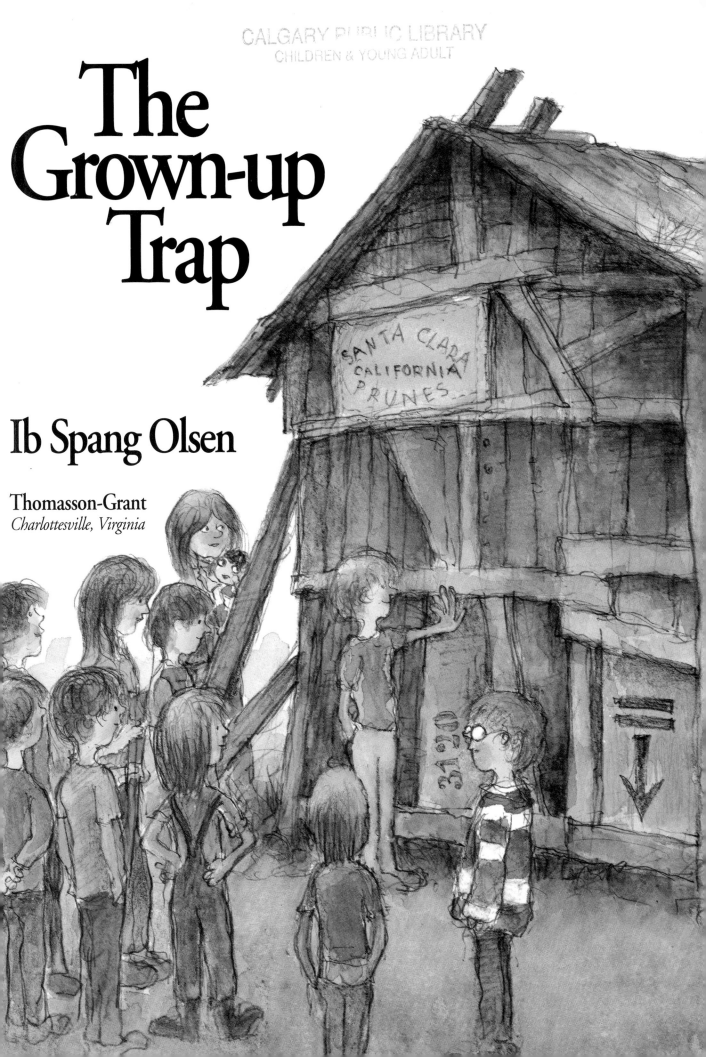

At breakfast, Caroline's mother and father
hardly ever say anything at all.
Caroline does most of the talking.

"Mom, I dreamt about you last night,"
she says. "You and I
were swinging in a hammock
for three whole days!"

"Imagine that," her mother says.
"Hurry up now and finish eating.
It's time for me to leave for work."

"I'd like to have another
piece of toast," Caroline says,
"with honey and peanut butter
and chocolate syrup . . ."

"Get up, Caroline,"
her father says.
"We'd better hurry,
or we'll be late, too."

"Bye-bye dear,"
her mother shouts
as she runs out the door.

At school
there's always
someone
to talk and
play with.
There's Polly
and Holly
and Leonard and John
and Wally and Frank
and Lisa and Don.

There's Kate and Paula,
too, but they're grown-ups
and they're so busy taking care
of all the children.

They don't have time
to sit down
and talk
with Caroline.

Caroline walks home
by herself.
She knows the way,
and she's always careful
crossing the street.

But she is full of questions.

Why are they digging that big hole?
What kind of bird is that?

I wish
I had someone here
to ask, she thinks.

Grown-ups know a lot,
Caroline says
to herself.
If I had a grown-up here,
I could find out
about everything.

Caroline is used to being alone
until her mother and father come home.
Sometimes she watches TV, and sometimes
she sees some very strange things.
I wouldn't mind having a grown-up here,
she thinks, right next to me.
Then I could find out what the shows
are all about.

Caroline's father
tells her a bedtime story
about some animals in the woods,
and then he says
good night.

"Stay a little longer,
won't you please?"
asks Caroline.

"I can't," her father says.
"I don't have time.
Sleep well, sweetheart."
And with that, he's gone.

I have plenty of time,
Caroline thinks.
If he had time, too,
I could tell him
about the animals
that live under my bed.

Early next morning,
Caroline wakes up in the middle of a dream.
With paper and crayons,
and before she forgets what it was all about,
she quickly finishes the story she was dreaming:

Lots of kids have pets like ducks
that waddle here and there.
Other kids like rabbits
if there's lots of room to spare.
A friend of mine keeps pigeons,
another keeps a parrot.
A cat will purr, a guinea pig
will munch a crunchy carrot.

A goat will eat most anything,
a dog will clean its dish
and wag its tail and run
and fetch the paper if you wish.
Bees will buzz into their hive
and make us honey for free.

But I'd prefer a grown-up
who is always there for me.

Grown-ups do just as they choose
unless we kids prevent it.
A trick to change the way they act
is what I've just invented.
Cage them up like parakeets.
Don't let grown-ups run free.
Shut them in and lock the door,
be sure to hide the key.

Or off they'll rush to work or shop
or meet with someone new
to help them think up other things
they simply have to do.
Sometimes they only sit and stare
in front of their TV,
as if that could ever be more fun
than spending time with me.

I've lots of boards and lots of nails,
and all my friends are willing,
to do a little hammering,
some sawing and some drilling.
And build a little wooden house
that looks just like a cozy den
and not at all like what it is,
a trap to keep them in.

They'll think it's just for grown-ups.
We'll make some signs that say:
"Come see free films and videos.
All kids must stay away!"
When they go in, the door will slam
and then they'll be really stuck.
So when they say they want to leave,
we'll say, "You're out of luck!"

FREE
POP
corn

Free
films

They'll scream and shout and pull their hair,
and some will stamp their feet,
but they will quiet down again
when we bring them things to eat.
And if we're kind, before too long
they're certain to grow tame
and settle down and come to us
when we call out their names.

I'll pick one out to be my own
then I'll unchain its leg
and give it treats and pat its head
and never make it beg.
Then it will tell me stories
and play with me all day,
and I will have a grown-up
who'll never run away.

It will read me lots of books,
then let me ask for more.
It might go walking on its hands
right through the open door!
And if I want to, it will let
me sit upon its knee

for hour after hour,
just my grown-up pet and me.

And when the night is thundery
and the sky is full of lightning,
with the two of us together,
it won't be half so frightening.

Then one sunny morning
when I'm sure my pet is tame,
I'll let it out, and hand in hand
we'll walk along the lane.

We'll find ourselves a park
or woods, a place that's far away

from all the things that ever make
a grown-up need to stray.

It will answer all the questions
that pop into my head
about the birds or trees
or something funny that I read.

For if you catch a grown-up,
and if you treat it right,
it will stay beside you all day long
and most of every night.
It will play and tell you jokes
and hug you when you're blue.
So trap yourself a grown-up—
it's the smartest thing to do!

"That's a good story,"
Caroline's friends say
when they hear it. "It might be fun
to catch a grown-up or two."

So they all start looking
for the things they need
to build a grown-up trap.

Grown-ups walking by stop to watch them
as they work. "See those children
playing," they say. "Aren't they sweet!"

At last the day comes
when the trap is finished.

The children think
it might be every bit
as good as the one
in Caroline's dream.

It's time to try it out!
They hide behind it
and wait for it to snare
a grown-up.

FREE
FILMS

GROWN
UPS
ONLY

FREE
MOVIES
AROUND
THE
CLOCK

IN
THIS WAY

FREE

Will they catch one?
And if they do, will this turn out
like Caroline's dream? Maybe then
they won't need a trap anymore.

Then together the grown-ups and children can make the little wooden house into something for them all to share.

Published by Thomasson-Grant, Inc.
Copyright © 1990 Ib Spang Olsen. Original title:
Voksenfælden. First published by Gyldendal,
Copenhagen. Published in agreement with ICBS,
Skindergade 3 B, DK-1159 Copenhagen K, Denmark

98 97 96 95 94 93 92   5 4 3 2 1

Any inquiries should be directed to
Thomasson-Grant, Inc.
One Morton Drive, Suite 500
Charlottesville, Virginia 22901
(804) 977-1780

Library of Congress Cataloging-in-Publication Data

Olsen, Ib Spang
      [Voksenfælden. English]
      The grown-up trap / Ib Spang Olsen.
              p.   cm.
      Translation of: Voksenfælden.
              Summary: Caroline wishes that her parents
      would spend more time with her and, in a dream,
      she comes up with an unusual idea about how to
      make this happen.
              ISBN 0-934738-96-3
              [1. Parent and child—Fiction. 2. Imagination—
      Fiction.]
      I. Title.
      PZ7.051755Gr   1992
      [E]—dc20 91-35251

                                                      CIP
                                                      AC

PRINTED IN BELGIUM BY
INTERNATIONAL BOOK PRODUCTION

THOMASSON-GRANT